Creaky Castle

# Tom's Dragon Trouble

## Tony Bradman

### Illustrated by
### Stephen Parkhouse

USBORNE

For everyone at Malcolm Primary School,
Penge's finest – and the place where I started...

*Tony Bradman*

First published in the UK in 2007 by Usborne Publishing Ltd., Usborne
House, 83-85 Saffron Hill, London EC1N 8RT, England. www.usborne.com

Text copyright © Tony Bradman, 2007
Illustration copyright © Usborne Publishing Ltd., 2007

A CIP catalogue record for this book is available from the British Library.

JFM MJJASOND/07
ISBN 9780746072271
Printed in Great Britain.

Contents

# Chapter One

# The King's Message

Thomas Bailey was beginning to feel more than a *teensy* bit frustrated.

He was having lunch with his family in the Great Hall of their ancestral home, Creaky Castle. But as usual, Thomas just couldn't seem to get a word in edgeways. Sir John and Lady Eleanor and his big sister Matilda were all far too busy talking to take any notice of *him*.

"Mother, I was wondering if I could—" Thomas started to say.

"Ugh, what *is* this foul muck?" said Matilda. She wrinkled her nose and poked at the food on her plate. "You can't possibly expect me to eat it. I mean, not even Mott would eat anything *this* awful, would you, Mott?"

Matilda offered a forkful of food to the family's ancient wolfhound. Mott sniffed it, whined...and slunk off to a distant corner of the hall.

"I'll thank you not to wave your food about, Matilda," said Lady Eleanor. "It's not *that* bad. Cook has made a special effort today."

Thomas took a deep breath and tried again. "Father, there's, er—"

"Really?" said Matilda, talking across him. "What, to poison us?"

"Oh no, I don't think so, my lambkin," said Sir John, smiling at her. "Cook wouldn't do anything like that. Well, not on purpose, anyway."

"HEY, WILL SOMEBODY LISTEN TO *ME*?" Thomas shouted.

"There's no need to be so *loud*, Thomas," said Lady Eleanor, wincing.

"It's vulgar, and you know how much I hate raised voices."

"Huh, except when *she's* doing the shouting," muttered Matilda.

"I heard that," snapped Lady Eleanor. "I *never* shout, except when it's absolutely necessary, of course. Which it often is with the inhabitants of this castle, sadly enough. Now, Thomas, what exactly is on your mind?"

"I was wondering if I could, er...have a pet," Thomas said nervously. "I was down in the village this morning, and I saw something I want at Peasant Pet Stores. It's on special offer, a really amazing bargain, and I've got enough money saved, so you wouldn't have to pay a penny..."

"Well, I don't see why not," said Sir John. "A boy needs a pet."

"Oh, great, Father, thanks!" said Thomas, amazed that it had been so easy after all. "I'll go and get...I mean, I'll go and buy him right away!"

"Hang on a second," said Lady Eleanor, looking

at Thomas through narrowed eyes. He paused half out of his seat, caught in her gaze, and slowly sat down again. "I notice you didn't mention what kind of animal it is you're in such a hurry to buy," said Lady Eleanor. "I'm afraid I'm going to need more detail before I give *my* permission, young man."

"It's a, er...dragon," Thomas said, practically whispering the word.

"A *dragon*?" said Lady Eleanor, frowning. "No, Thomas, definitely not. They're nasty, dangerous beasts, and they eat colossal amounts of food."

"Oh no, we definitely can't afford any high-maintenance pets," Sir John said hastily. "We've been spending rather too much recently as it is."

"I feel another cut in pocket money coming on," Matilda groaned.

Thomas opened his mouth to argue with his parents. But at that precise moment, the doors of the Great Hall were suddenly flung wide open and a short, rather squat soldier came running in. It was Mouldy, Sir John's senior man-at-arms. Mouldy

13

hurried towards the table, almost tripping over his sword a couple of times, and skidded to a halt beside Sir John.

"Sorry to interrupt your lovely lunch, My Lord," he said breathlessly, "but a knight has brought a message for you. What shall I do with him?"

"That should be obvious, Mouldy," sighed Sir John. "Send him in!"

"But dragons *aren't* nasty *or* dangerous," Thomas went on, as Mouldy scuttled out. "They can be very loving and loyal, and they often–"

"Read my lips, Thomas," said Mother. "*The...answer...is...NO.*"

Thomas scowled, determined not to give up. But then he heard hoofs clip-clopping up

flagstone steps, and a tall knight in splendid
armour burst into the Great Hall on his horse.
Mouldy came stumbling in
after him.

The knight leaned down from the saddle, handed Sir John a rolled parchment, then, without a word, swung his horse round and clattered out again.

"How many times have I told you to make them leave their horses in the stables?" Lady Eleanor hissed at Mouldy, who turned and fled. "I don't know why we bother to have any stables at all," Lady Eleanor muttered. "No one ever uses them." She turned to her husband. "Well?"

"It's from the King..." said Sir John. "He's, er... coming to visit."

"*WHAT?*" squealed Lady Eleanor, horrified. "When does he arrive?"

"Next Monday," Sir John said gloomily. "He'll only be staying a few days, thank goodness, so we probably shouldn't make much fuss."

"Don't be ridiculous!" said Lady Eleanor. "We'll have to redecorate the entire castle, of course. We'll need new furniture and hangings in here and in the bedchambers, new outfits for us, and for the servants, too. In fact, we might need to get some new servants. *Especially* a new cook."

"I hope you're not expecting me to wear a horrid pointy hat, or some hideous *snood*," Matilda muttered, her top lip curled in disgust. "I mean, it's bad enough having to go round in stupid girly dresses all the time."

"You will if I say so," said Lady Eleanor. "And another thing..."

"Could we get back to what we were talking about?" said Thomas.

"I'm not sure we can afford to redecorate the *entire* castle," murmured Sir John. "It's a big job, and as I say, money *is* a bit of an issue..."

"But we have to!" said Lady Eleanor. "And *you* have to make a good impression on the King. If everything goes well, he might promote you. We wouldn't have to worry about money if you were a rich baron."

"Oh dear," said Sir John, sighing and looking unhappy. "I really don't think I'm up to it, my love. It all sounds a little too energetic for me – you know I like a nice, quiet life. Can't we, er... just stay as we are?"

Lady Eleanor went onto the attack, Matilda sided with Sir John, and Thomas realized he had less chance now than ever of being listened to.

"May I get down from the table?" he asked, but didn't wait for an answer. He left the Great Hall, emerged from the Keep, crossed the empty courtyard...then slipped through a back door into the stables.

And there, hidden in a heap of old straw, was the small dragon – well, smallish – that Thomas had already bought and sneaked into Creaky Castle.

Buying the dragon first and asking permission later had seemed like a brilliant idea at the time. But now Thomas wasn't so sure.

"Are you all right, Sparky?" Thomas whispered. A woeful noise came in reply, a cross between a cow mooing and the purring of a giant cat. "Sorry, but I might have to keep you hidden here for a while longer," Thomas said. "If Mother finds out what I've done, I'll be in *big* trouble. In fact, I don't even want to think about how much trouble I'll be in..."

Sad little puffs of smoke emerged from the heap of straw. Thomas stood there brooding, wondering what to do. How could he persuade Mother to let him keep Sparky? Then suddenly it came to him...

Chapter Two

# Headless Chickens

"It's simple, Sparky," Thomas murmured. A big, green snout poked out of the straw. Thomas stroked it absent-mindedly, and Sparky purred softly with pleasure. "I just need to help Father impress the King, that's all..."

Thomas had realized that if the King *did* make Father a rich baron, they would have more than enough money to feed a dragon, however much it might cost. Although Thomas didn't believe it could be *that* expensive. Mother wouldn't be able to complain, anyway. And once she got to know Sparky, she would see how wonderful having a pet dragon could be.

"It won't be easy," said Thomas, thinking about Sir John. "Between you and me, Father isn't terribly impressive at the best of times. But I'm sure I can come up with something. Listen, Sparky, I'd better be off. See you later, okay? And don't worry, I *will* bring you some food, I promise."

Thomas quietly slipped out of the stable block and started making his way back towards the Keep, whistling cheerfully as he sauntered along. But he soon noticed that the courtyard was no longer empty. Now it was full of harassed-looking servants and anxious men-at-arms, all of them scampering around and bumping into each other like headless chickens.

Thomas caught a glimpse of his sister and ran across to her. "What's going on, Matilda?" he said. She had changed out of the dress she'd been wearing earlier and into her favourite outfit, a chain-mail shirt and helmet.

"Huh, what do you think?" said Matilda. "Mother's started giving orders to everybody right, left and centre, so I'm off before she catches me. And if I were you, little brother, I'd stay well out of her way, too."

"THOMAS!" Mother yelled, her voice ringing out across the courtyard like a trumpet. Thomas froze instantly. "I've got a little job for you..."

"Too late!" laughed Matilda, pulling down her visor to hide her face. Then she was gone. Thomas sighed, and trudged off towards Mother.

He discovered the "little job" was actually quite a big one, and more were to follow. Thomas had to tidy his bedchamber ("It's a disgrace," said Mother). Then he had to clean out the cupboards where he kept the interesting stuff he found in the woods, such as his collection of animal skulls and dead birds. ("We all have to make sacrifices, Thomas," Mother said when he complained.) And then he had to help Mouldy give Mott a bath, something Mott loathed. Thomas didn't enjoy it much, either.

So he wasn't able to even think about returning to the stable block until later in the evening, almost bedtime. And first he had to visit the kitchen.

"Can I take a few leftovers, Cook?" he said. "Er...for Mott, that is."

"Why not?" Cook moaned. He was sitting at a table, looking deeply depressed. "There are always plenty, after all. Tell me, Thomas, is my cooking *that* bad? Is Mott the only one in this castle who will eat my food? You know, sometimes I think there's no point in carrying on."

"Sorry, Cook, er...can't stop to chat," Thomas said uncomfortably, hurrying out with a sack of leftovers and scraps, remembering the way Mott had reacted when Matilda had offered him some of her lunch...

"I just hope you like this, Sparky," said Thomas, as he emptied the sack onto the stable floor. Thomas was worried Sparky would feel the same way as Mott about Cook's food, but he had no

idea what else to give him. So he was relieved –
and also quite surprised – when Sparky wolfed
down the lot, even the bones, then sat up with a
"More, please!" look in his big, green eyes. "Er...
good boy, Sparky," Thomas said uncertainly.

*

The next few days were rather difficult. Lady Eleanor was a woman on a mission. She gave endless instructions to everyone, and she relentlessly pursued the slow and the idle, especially her family. This made it very hard for Thomas to visit Sparky. Whenever he did manage to, he came away feeling nervous. Sparky gobbled up everything Thomas could bring him, yet still he seemed constantly hungry. And now Thomas realized Sparky was growing each day – almost with each mouthful.

Thomas was starting to think he'd have to get Sparky out of the stables soon, or he might never get him out at all. Where else could he hide him, though? He'd thought the stable block was perfect. As Mother had said, nobody ever went there. But it might attract more attention than usual if Sparky's tail was sticking out of the door, or his head through the roof...

"Cheer up, Tom," Sir John said one morning.

"I can't blame you for feeling a trifle glum, though. I wish none of this was happening myself."

Father, of course, was another problem. Thomas had been studying him, trying to come up with a

way of making him more impressive. But Sir John was short, plump and balding, and he rarely did anything... well, *manly*. He liked reading old manuscripts, and pottering around in his study, and was happiest when he could sneak off for a quiet afternoon of fishing in the moat. Thomas kept suggesting it might be a good idea for him to do some serious practice with his sword, or even just a little light jousting with the men-at-arms. Father, however, seemed not to hear.

In the end, Thomas decided his best bet was to do something about Sir John's appearance. There wasn't enough time to turn him into a fierce warrior – but with a bit of help he might at least *look* rather more warlike.

"Don't worry, Father, I'm fine," said Thomas. "By the way, have you had a chance yet to go through that catalogue I gave you yesterday?"

"Catalogue?" said Sir John. "I don't remember any catalogue."

"Doesn't the name *Mail Shots* sound familiar?" said Thomas. "Armour and weapons by post? You ought to have some new kit, you know, to impress the King. And I noticed that they do, er...large waist sizes."

"Oh yes, it's coming back to me," said Sir John. "Thanks, Tom. But I can't really afford to buy anything new at the moment, so I'll probably just polish up my old stuff. Although don't tell your mother I said that."

Sir John hurried off, and Thomas sighed. Now he was totally stumped.

He didn't have any more ideas, and time was swiftly running out...

# Chapter Three

# Blackened Little Corpse

It was Monday morning, and the inhabitants
of Creaky Castle were lined up in the sunny
courtyard, waiting for the King to arrive. Thomas
was standing in front with Matilda, Father
and Mott, the castle's men-at-arms and servants
behind them. Lady Eleanor was off checking
something.

Thomas nervously crossed his fingers behind
his back. He hoped Mother wasn't doing anything
that might lead her to Sparky. Thomas had at last

found another, safer hiding place for his growing dragon, a large, old storehouse in a quiet corner over by the northern wall. He had also managed to get Sparky out of the stables and across the courtyard in the middle of the night when no one was around. It had still felt very risky, though. And it had turned out to be a quite disturbing experience, too.

Thomas frowned. He had some idea now why dragons might have gained a reputation for being nasty and dangerous. A rat had scurried past them in the alley behind the stables. Thomas hadn't been bothered – there were always rats scuttling about Creaky Castle – but Sparky had been spooked. He had instantly reared up, opened his mouth, and fired off a terrific burst of flame. The rat hadn't stood a chance. Then Sparky had chuckled hoarsely, and slurped up the blackened little corpse. All of which had kind of made Thomas look at Sparky in a different way...

Suddenly another hoarse chuckle broke into Thomas's thoughts.

"Love the pageboy outfit, little brother," Matilda whispered. "Er...not! Those stripy leggings make you look even more bandy than you actually are."

"Huh, you can talk..." Thomas muttered under his breath, elbowing her. "Does your head go all the way to the top of that pointy hat?"

"Steady, children," hissed a red-faced Sir John. He was wearing full armour, and obviously feeling quite warm. "Here comes your mother!"

"Everything seems to be in order, amazingly enough," murmured Lady Eleanor, as she took her place beside the rest of her family. "Although perhaps I should have one more look around inside, just to make sure."

"If you like, dear," said Sir John. "But I don't think there's any need."

"Definitely not," muttered Thomas. Despite Father's protests, Mother had got all the new furniture and hangings she'd wanted, and the interior of Creaky Castle had been totally redecorated. Gone were the cobwebs, the tatty old tapestries, the battered beds and benches. In fact, the whole place was so perfect now it hardly seemed like their home any more.

"Are you sure my hair is all right?" said Lady Eleanor, patting it.

"I've already told you, dear," sighed Sir John. "You look wonderful."

"Stop worrying, Mother," said Matilda. "It's too late now, anyway."

"You're right, I must stay calm," said Lady Eleanor. "Deep breaths, *in* through the nose, *out* through the mouth... I just wish he'd get here."

Suddenly, a terrific shout went up in the gatehouse. Mouldy came dashing across the courtyard, almost tripping over his sword as usual.

"It's *him*!" he yelled, his eyes wide. "He's...he's ...in the village!"

"Well, lower the drawbridge, then, and let him in!" said Sir John.

Mouldy skidded to a halt, swivelled on his heel, and ran back to the gatehouse. Soon, Thomas could hear great winches groaning, and chains clanking, and a crash as the  drawbridge hit the ground, followed by the sound of iron-shod hooves thundering over its thick wooden planks.

"Here we go...smile everybody!" murmured Lady Eleanor. She turned to her husband. "I forgot to ask...you *did* hire a new cook, didn't you?"

"Ah, no, well, actually..." Sir John muttered, "I, er...didn't. Cook gets so depressed, and I thought it would probably have broken his heart..."

"I *don't* believe it..." said Lady Eleanor, the colour draining from her face. "You mean to tell me that the food will be...*the same as usual*?"

"I'm sure it won't matter," said Sir John. "Er... not much, anyway."

Mother glared, and Matilda giggled. Thomas focused his attention on the group of mounted knights clattering across the courtyard towards them. They made a fine sight, their armour glinting in the sunlight as they came to a halt. A herald jumped from his horse and blew his trumpet.

"HEAR YE, HEAR YE!" he yelled. "I hereby announce the arrival of His Royal Magnificence King Stephen The First And Only, Lord of—"

"Yes, yes, that will do," said a portly figure

getting off his own horse and waving the herald away. Thomas realized this was the King. "We'll be here for hours if he goes through *all* my titles," the King added.

"Welcome to Creaky Castle, My Lord!"
said Lady Eleanor, curtsying. "I can't tell you
how excited we are Your Majesty has come to
visit us..."

Lady Eleanor rattled on, Sir John joining in when she nudged him, but Thomas didn't bother to listen to the grown-ups. Instead, he let his eyes roam over the men on horseback. Thomas realized they must be the King's bodyguard, each of them tall, grim-faced and tough-looking, and wearing the same armour as the knight who had brought the message. It was a good job he'd moved Sparky, he thought. Mother was bound to insist their horses be kept in the stables while they were at Creaky Castle.

Suddenly, Thomas heard growling, and glanced down. Mott was staring at one of the men, his teeth bared. Thomas was surprised. It was strange behaviour for Mott, an old softy who usually liked everyone. Thomas examined the man more closely. He saw a neat black beard, thin lips and cruel eyes, the man's gaze boring into the back of the King's neck.

"I'd like to be shown to my chamber now, Bailey," said the King. "You can sort out the security arrangements with the captain of my bodyguard, Baron de Rathbone." He nodded in the direction of the man Thomas had been studying, and the baron nodded in return. But he didn't smile.

"Of course, My Lord," said Sir John. "If you'd care to follow me."

"Lead on, Bailey," said the King. "I trust you've got a good lunch lined up for us. I love my food, and I can be very fussy, can't I, de Rathbone?"

Lady Eleanor let out a squeak, but Thomas took no notice. A tingling in his skin told him something about Baron de Rathbone wasn't right.

Thomas had already decided to keep a very close eye on him...

# Chapter Four

# A Plot Discovered

Lunch was, of course, a *total* disaster. The Great Hall was packed with the King and his knights, and Thomas had never seen so many people looking so disgusted at the same time. They all stared disbelievingly at the charred, gooey mess on their plates, and no one ate a single morsel.

"What exactly is it supposed to *be*?" complained the King at last.

"Er...overcooked underwear by the look of it,"

Matilda whispered. She grinned at her brother, and they both spluttered with laughter.

Lady Eleanor glared at them, then turned to the King and smiled. "I'm sorry, Your Majesty," she said brightly. "It must be some kind of mistake. If you'll excuse me, I'll pop into the kitchen and see what's going on. My husband will keep you entertained meanwhile – won't you, *dear*?"

"What, me?" murmured Sir John. "Oh, yes, whatever you say, my love. Er...perhaps I could give you a tour of our humble abode, My Lord."

"I'd rather have a decent lunch," grumbled the King. He looked very grumpy. "I'm so hungry my stomach thinks my throat has been cut."

Some instinct made Thomas glance at the baron. He saw de Rathbone's mouth twitch into a faint – but definite – smirk at the King's words. De Rathbone also reached for his dagger, and seemed to grip the hilt tightly.

Thomas wondered what all that was about. Umm, very interesting...

"I'm sure Lady Eleanor will sort things out, My Lord," Sir John was saying. "Er...in fact I think I can hear her doing it even as we speak."

Everyone paused to listen. Strange sounds were coming from behind the door that led to the kitchen – muffled yelling, lots of crashes, pleas for mercy. Matilda and Thomas looked at each other and rolled their eyes.

"Oh well, I suppose a bit of a wait will make me appreciate lunch all the more when I get it," sighed the King. "See to the men, de Rathbone."

"At your service, My Lord," the baron growled, the smirk replaced now by a stiff, wintry smile that sent a chill down Thomas's spine.

"We could start with a walk on the battlements, Your Majesty," said Sir John, as he ushered the King out. He looked over his shoulder at Thomas and Matilda. "See if your mother needs any help!" he mouthed at them.

"Huh, he has *got* to be joking," muttered Matilda, removing her hat and dumping it on top of her lunch. "I'm off, little brother. See you later."

With that, she dashed up the stairs that led to the bedchambers. Thomas barely registered her departure. He was busy keeping an eye on Baron de Rathbone, who was giving orders to the knights. They trooped out after the King, probably heading for the barrack block, Thomas thought.

Then he noticed that not all the knights had left. Two had stayed with de Rathbone, and the three men went into a huddle in the furthest corner of the Great Hall. Thomas hung back, hoping to hear what they were going to say. But de Rathbone and the knights kept scowling over their shoulders, and he realized they were waiting for him to leave, too. That made him even more determined to eavesdrop, and he knew just how.

Thomas stood up and strolled out under their narrow-eyed gaze. But the instant he was in the courtyard he ran round to a door on the other side of the Keep. He slipped inside, dashed up a narrow staircase, entered a gallery above the Great Hall and crept along the floor. He stopped by the balustrade, cautiously raised his head, and looked down. The baron and the knights were in the same place, de Rathbone talking quietly.

"At last, the moment I have been waiting for draws near," he said, his voice trembling with excitement. "As soon as we arrived in this shoddy little castle I knew it was the place where I would achieve my destiny."

*Shoddy little castle?* thought Thomas. How dare the baron say such a thing! De Rathbone had better not let Mother hear him talk like that, or he would be in more trouble than he could handle.

But de Rathbone hadn't finished. He ranted on about how much he hated and resented the King.

"Why, not even his own parents liked him!" the baron said at last. "Do you know, he told me once in a weak moment – and in confidence, of course – that his family nickname was *Porky* because he was such a greedy boy? How can you respect anyone who tells you something like that?" The two knights laughed, and agreed with him. "Anyway, tonight we strike," de Rathbone went on, "and tomorrow...*I* will be King!"

"Hail to the new King!" the knights said, each one crashing a mailed fist against his armoured chest. De Rathbone returned their salute.

Thomas had almost stopped listening, his mind suddenly full of a strange vision of the King as a plump, unhappy little boy... But now he gulped, and felt himself going cold all over. De Rathbone could only become the new King if the old one was...dead. Thomas had just overheard a plot to kill King Stephen!

"You know what you have to do?" de Rathbone was saying now.

"Aye, My Lord," whispered one of the knights. "We are to keep watch at the door to the King's bedchamber while you are, er...dealing with him."

"Quite so," said de Rathbone, smirking again. "It won't take long."

"But what about the rest of the King's men, My Lord?" said the other knight. "And the Baileys – what are you going to do with them?"

Thomas held his breath, and felt his heart almost skip a beat.

"Oh, don't worry, I'm pretty sure I know how to make the bodyguard come over to me," de Rathbone said. "But as for the Baileys...well, Sir John is a fat buffoon, his ghastly wife seems to spend her whole time squawking like a demented hen, and those children are obviously just a pair of idiot brats. So I think I'll simply have them all put to death. Now, I wish to see the King's chamber while he is otherwise engaged..."

Thomas watched as de Rathbone and the knights strode across the Great Hall and tramped upstairs. Then he let out his breath and ducked down again. He felt absolutely furious with de Rathbone after listening to him say such nasty stuff about his family, and decided then and there to tell his parents and the King what he'd heard. That would soon put a stop to de Rathbone's plotting! He turned and ran quietly along the gallery, down the staircase and emerged into the courtyard. Then he suddenly skidded to a halt.

He'd just had the most wonderful idea, one so shockingly brilliant he could hardly believe he'd come up with it himself. Something that would make the King think Father was *really* impressive.

Thomas was going to arrange for Father to save the King's life.

# Chapter Five

# A Burst
# of Flame

Thomas stood in the courtyard for a moment, his mind racing. He could see it all. Father waiting in the King's chamber to stop de Rathbone, the grateful King making Father a rich baron on the spot, Mother beaming happily at Thomas and saying that he could have any pet he wanted now they were so rich, even a pet dragon, why not have two, or three, or...

"THOMAS!" said a loud voice. He almost jumped out of his skin, and turned to see a

51

grim-faced Lady Eleanor advancing towards him. "Why are you standing there with that stupid grin on your face? Don't you realize we're in the middle of an emergency? Where's your father?"

"Er...on the battlements with the King, I think," said Thomas.

"Well, I want you to go and tell him that I've made an executive decision," said Mother. "I've fired Cook, so we're having a takeaway this evening whether your father thinks we can afford it or not. I've sent Mouldy to pick up 500 pies at Pudding Express. Hang on a moment..."

Mother marched across the courtyard and came to a halt near the back door of the stables. She glared at a large black scorch mark on the wall.

"What...is...*THIS*?" she said. "It looks as if someone's had a bonfire here. *You* don't happen to know anything about it, do you, Thomas?"

"Me?" squeaked Thomas. "Of course not, Mother. Why would I?"

"Oh, I don't know," said Mother, frowning at him.

"Let's just call it a parent's intuition. I'm warning
you, Thomas, you'd better not be up to any
mischief – I've got enough on my plate as it is.
Now run along and find your father. I'll have to
get one of the servants to clean this wall."

Thomas scurried off, relieved to escape for the
time being, although now he felt rather uneasy.
Mother obviously suspected he was up to
*something*, and that might turn out to be very
dangerous indeed for him. She was pretty stressed,
and Thomas dreaded to think what she would do
if she found out about Sparky before he managed
to make everything right. He felt
sorry for Cook, too, although
he wasn't that surprised.

Thomas delivered
the message about
the takeaway,
whispering it to
Father so the King
wouldn't hear.

Father went pale, but Thomas slipped away, keen to check on Sparky and take him some leftovers. When he got to the kitchen he discovered that Cook had refused to leave, even though Lady Eleanor had fired him. He had locked himself in the pantry instead, where Thomas could hear him sobbing noisily.

There was deep silence at Sparky's hiding place, though. Thomas glanced over his shoulder. Nobody was around, so he pushed open one of the big double doors just a crack and slipped through. It was dark inside, and at first Thomas could make out nothing but the vaguest of shapes.

"Hey, Sparky!" he said. He dropped the sack of leftovers on the floor and went in a little further. "Sparky, where are you?" he said more loudly.

He heard Sparky's familiar purring, although it seemed much noisier than usual. Thomas peered in the direction it was coming from...and saw a pair of large, glowing, green ovals hovering in mid-air high above him. There was a small pair of red circles below them, too. As Thomas watched, the red circles abruptly grew much bigger and redder, and a burst of flame shot out of them, lighting up the entire storehouse.

"Oh, wow..." said Thomas, his jaw dropping in surprise.

Thomas saw that his pet dragon had grown, well...quite a lot. His head was almost as high as the storehouse's roof beams, and his tail twice the length of his massive body. The green ovals were Sparky's eyes, the red circles his nostrils, the burst of flame similar to the one that had roasted the rat, but much more powerful and longer lasting. It stopped as abruptly as it had started, and deep darkness filled the storehouse again.

Suddenly, Thomas felt very small – and rather nervous. He could sense the massive bulk of Sparky moving swiftly towards him, hear his claws scraping across the storehouse floor. Thomas backed off, but it was too late. Sparky's head loomed out of the darkness, his eyes still glowing green, and Thomas thought he was doomed to the same fate as the rat. He closed his own eyes and waited for the scorching flame to envelop him.

But Sparky only nuzzled against him, the dragon's scaly skin feeling warm and giving off a smoky smell. Thomas opened his eyes and realized that Sparky still loved him, even though the small dragon he'd bought was now pretty big. Thomas grinned and happily hugged his pet, or at least tried to. His arms only just went round Sparky's snout.

"Good boy, Sparky," he murmured. Sparky purred back at him. "But how did you get to be this size? What have you been eating in here?"

Thomas soon had the answer to both questions. He found an old torch in a wall brazier and got Sparky to light it, which was a scary experience.

Thomas immediately saw that the storehouse was where Creaky Castle's food supplies were kept and Sparky had been helping himself. Thomas hadn't taken any notice of the heaps of sacks and

rows of barrels when he'd put Sparky in there the night before. At the time, the only thing on his mind had been finding a safer hiding place for his pet.

He'd been incredibly lucky no one had come to the storehouse that day – Cook must have taken everything he needed for the King's visit the evening before. And now Cook wasn't going to be doing any cooking, so Sparky might be safe in the storehouse for a while longer. But if he kept growing at this rate there wouldn't be anywhere at all to hide him, and no food left for anyone.

Thomas stood watching Sparky slurp up the leftovers he'd brought, and wondered if he shouldn't just admit to Mother what he'd done and get it over with. He could tell her and Father about the baron's plot at the same time. But de Rathbone would deny it, of course, and Thomas knew Mother would then be cross with *him* for being rude to a guest. And that would mean she'd be even more likely to make him get rid of Sparky.

"It looks like I'd better stick to my plan, Sparky," Thomas said. Sparky made his woeful, half-mooing, half-purring noise again. "I know, I'm worried about it myself," Thomas murmured, stroking Sparky's huge snout. "I'm not sure Father is up to it. But he'll have to be, I suppose..."

Thomas would have to do his best to turn Father into a hero.

# Chapter Six

# Caught in the Act

"I don't understand, Tom," muttered Father, struggling to sit up in bed. "The King wants me to come to his chamber now? But why? It's so late."

"Please, Father, keep your voice down," Thomas hissed. He was standing beside his parents' bed, still wearing his day clothes, the hideous outfit Mother had made him wear, his flickering candle the only light in their darkened chamber. "You don't want to wake Mother, do you?"

"No, of course not!" Sir John whispered,

nervously glancing at the sleeping form of his wife beside him. Her eyes were covered by a mask, and her hair was in curlers. "Not after the day she's had, poor thing."

At that moment, Lady Eleanor twitched and moaned. Thomas thought she was probably having nightmares about all that had happened, and felt sorry for her. The pies from Pudding Express had been awful. They had taken ages to arrive, the pastry had been like old shoe leather, and the only filling left had been Spicy Boar, which the King didn't like.

"Come on, Father, get a move on," Thomas whispered. "The King just said he needs to see you, and I'm sure he hates being kept waiting. Oh, and, er...I think you'd better put on your armour, and bring your sword."

"Do I have to?" Father groaned. "It was such a relief to take it off and put on my nightshirt." He got out of bed, but then he stopped. "Hey, wait a minute," he said, frowning at him. "How come the King sent *you* with the message, and not one of his men? You should be in bed, my lad..."

Thomas took a deep breath. He'd thought Father would ask a few awkward questions, so he'd worked out some answers in advance, and had rehearsed them while waiting in his own chamber for everyone to go to bed. He had wanted to be certain that Mother was asleep – there was no way he could have dealt with lots of difficult questions from her as well.

"You must have shut Mott in the courtyard when you came to bed," Thomas whispered. That was plausible, he thought. Father always checked the doors of the Keep at bedtime, and he *did* sometimes lock Mott out. "I heard him whining, and I went downstairs to let him in."

"Oh dear," said Father, his frown changing into a look of shame. "I'm sorry, Thomas. I was a bit distracted earlier. What a good boy you are."

"Anyway, I was just going past the King's chamber on my way back to bed when he opened his door and, er...ordered me to fetch you," said Thomas. "His men are all sleeping in the barrack block, aren't they?"

"Forgive me for doubting you, Thomas," said

Father. "Now, you'll have to help me with my armour. Although maybe I'll just take my helmet and sword. I don't want to be *too* formal. It *is* the middle of the night..."

"Er...whatever," Thomas whispered. "Can we just get going?"

Thomas felt a twinge of guilt as he hurried Father down the torchlit corridors towards the King's chamber. After all, he had told some pretty big fibs, and Father had been nice, as usual. But being nice had never got Father very far, and Thomas felt he was being untruthful for a good cause.

His plan was simple. He still wasn't going to tell Father about the plot. He would just make sure Father was in the King's chamber when the baron turned up. That might be enough to stop de Rathbone by itself. But Thomas would raise the alarm in any case, to be on the safe side. Then Creaky Castle's men-at-arms and the King's bodyguard would come running, and it would all be over – and Sir John would be a hero.

Thomas only hoped he and Father made it to the King's chamber in time. It had occurred to him earlier that he had no idea when de Rathbone actually planned to strike. Thomas had worried about it, then decided that like him, the baron would probably wait until everyone else was asleep before he made his move. So there really wasn't a moment to lose.

At last they came to the door of the King's chamber. Thomas paused in the shadows at the end of the corridor, looked both ways...and gave a sigh of relief. There was no sign of de Rathbone or his two henchmen.

"What are we waiting for, Thomas?" whispered a puzzled Sir John.

"Er...nothing, Father," said Thomas, heading for the King's door.

He stopped before it, listened for a second, then gripped the iron ring and pushed. The door slowly swung open with a creak of rusty hinges.

"Oh, Thomas!" hissed Sir John. "You should have knocked first!"

Thomas ignored him and peered into the chamber. It was pitch-black inside, so Thomas boldly walked in and held up his candle. If the King was awake, Thomas was ready with a

story for him. He was going to say that Father was simply making sure he was all right – and hope that de Rathbone would arrive soon. But Thomas could see that the King was lying flat out in bed. He was fast asleep, and snoring rather loudly, too.

"Psst, Thomas!" Father hissed nervously behind him. "I think we'd better leave. The King obviously doesn't want to see me after all."

"No!" whispered Thomas, panicking. He had to get Father to stay. "I'm sure he does," he said. "Er...he must have fallen asleep waiting..."

"Well, what do you expect me to do now?" Father whispered, an edge of irritation creeping into his voice. "I can't wake him up, can I?"

"We should, er...just hang around for a while," said Thomas, thinking fast. "Why don't you hide...I mean, *stand* over there, behind the door?"

At that moment the King muttered and Sir John hurried over to him. He halted by the bed and stood to attention, his sword raised in a salute.

"Your Majesty," he murmured, "please forgive this intrusion, but..."

Suddenly, the door behind them creaked open again, and the chamber was flooded with torchlight. Thomas turned...and saw de Rathbone and his two henchmen standing in the doorway, the baron's face a mask of surprise. But de Rathbone recovered before Thomas could say a word.

"Hah, caught in the act!" yelled the baron. "Seize the assassins, men!"

"But that's not right!" said Thomas. "We're not the assassins, you–"

Thomas wasn't allowed to finish his sentence. De Rathbone's knights grabbed them both, and bundled them out of the chamber.

# Chapter Seven

# A Family on Trial

Thomas sat on the floor in the corner of the cell where he had spent an uncomfortable night. Creaky Castle's dungeons hadn't been used for years – even Mother had forgotten about them – and they were dank, cobwebby and smelly. Thomas had barely slept, and now it was morning, the sunlight peeping through the bars of the tiny window above him.

He was desperate to know what was happening to Father, and to Mother and Matilda, too. He and

Father had been separated from each other by
de Rathbone and his men. Then Thomas had been
thrown into a cell on his own, and the knight
standing guard in the corridor – one of the King's
men – had steadfastly refused
to answer any of
his questions.

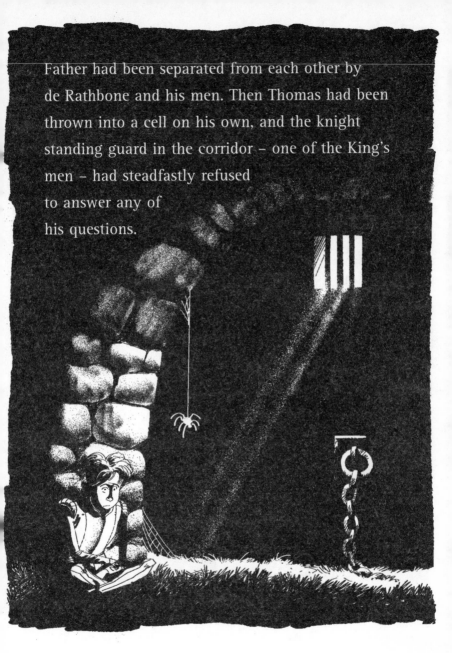

Well, if at first you don't succeed, Thomas thought, and rose to his feet, intending to pound on the door and shout at the knight outside. But then he heard heavy footsteps thudding towards the dungeon. A key rattled in the lock, the door was flung open, and Thomas saw that the corridor beyond was filled with more men from the King's bodyguard.

"Right, come with us," growled the knight in front. Thomas recognized him as a henchman of de Rathbone. "And no funny business, or else..."

"I'm not going anywhere until I know exactly what you've done with my father," said Thomas, crossing his arms and scowling. "And just you wait till I tell my mother about all this, she's going to be *so* cross..."

But the knight only grunted and dragged Thomas from the dungeon by the scruff of his neck. Then he frogmarched him into the courtyard, the other knights tramping grimly behind. Sir John and Lady Eleanor and

Matilda were already there, and Thomas was very
relieved to see that they all seemed unharmed,
although Matilda and Mother were both in their
nightdresses, and Mother still had curlers in her
hair. Father was wearing his nightshirt and
helmet, but he didn't have his sword any more.

De Rathbone was standing over them, an
arrogant smirk on his face. Next to him was the
King, sitting on Father's chair from the Great Hall
as if it were his throne, and looking incredibly
grumpy. Some of his men had their swords drawn
and were watching Sir John, Lady Eleanor and
Matilda. Others were holding back an angry
crowd of the Baileys' men-at-arms and servants.
Thomas could see Mouldy at the front, yelling and
jostling the King's knights, and shaking his fist at
de Rathbone.

Things were looking bad for the Baileys, and
Thomas was a little worried, to say the least – and
feeling perhaps just a *teensy* bit guilty, too. He had
done a lot of thinking during his night in the

dungeon, and he had begun to feel that maybe he should have told his parents about de Rathbone's plot after all. And also that he shouldn't have tried to get Father involved.

It was no good telling them now, though. Thomas was certain Mother would go absolutely

berserk if she found out what he'd been up to, and
of course then she wouldn't let him keep Sparky,
not in a million years. He would just have to
swallow the guilt. Besides, he was convinced he
could still come up with a way out of this mess.
*If* he kept his nerve, that is...

"Thomas, thank heavens!" Mother cried out when she saw him. "Are you all right?" She and Father gave him a big hug, and Matilda joined in.

But then Lady Eleanor took a step back, held Thomas at arm's length, and drew in her breath sharply. "Why, this is absolutely outrageous! What on earth have you done to my son, de Rathbone, you brute?" she said, rounding furiously on the baron. "*His new outfit is completely ruined!*"

"Bad luck, Tommy," said Matilda. "You looked so good in it, too."

"Ha ha, very funny...I don't think," Thomas whispered, and moved closer to her. "Are you okay? What did they do to you and Mother?"

"Same as you," Matilda whispered in reply. "Shoved us in dungeons, but on the other side of the Keep. I think they held Father in the hall..."

"Never mind his new outfit," growled Sir John, glaring at the baron. "I'm warning you, de Rathbone, if you or your men have harmed

even a single hair on this boy's head, I promise
you'll pay dearly. I know I don't look like much
of a knight, but no one hurts my family and gets
away with it. And I mean *no one.*
Have I made myself
perfectly clear?"

"Oh, I say, Sir John," murmured Lady Eleanor, moving closer to him and squeezing his arm. "I'd forgotten just how...*forceful* you can be."

"Really?" said Sir John, blushing and smiling bashfully at her. Then he squared his shoulders. "I suppose it *was* rather impressive, wasn't it?"

"Oh please, let's have no ghastly *lovey-dovey* stuff," the baron sneered. "I might throw up... You can spare me the pathetic threats too,

 Bailey. They don't work, and you're in no position to make them, anyway."

"Can we start now, de Rathbone?" whined the King. "I've had no breakfast yet, so I'd like to get this trial finished as soon as possible."

"*Trial?*" snapped Lady Eleanor. "The only person who should be on trial is that stupid man," she hissed, giving de Rathbone one of her full-strength glares. Thomas was amazed the baron wasn't instantly reduced to a heap of ashes. "I have never been so insulted, Your Majesty," Lady Eleanor continued. "Pulled from my bed in the middle of the night, denied access to a hairbrush and clean clothes, and all because that...*numbskull* claims Sir John wanted to kill you. Which is completely ridiculous!"

"Go, Mother!" said Matilda, adding her glare to those of her parents. Thomas thought he'd better do a spot of glaring himself, and joined in.

"But I'm not a vindictive woman," said Lady Eleanor, treating the King to one of her most charming smiles. "And I would be quite happy to forgive and forget, as long as we can put all this nonsense behind us—"

"*SILENCE, WOMAN!*" roared de Rathbone. "My men and I caught Bailey standing over the

King with his sword drawn. Didn't we, men?"

"Aye, My Lord," said one of the henchmen. "It was just as you say."

"But...but I was only saluting His Majesty," spluttered Sir John.

"And besides," Lady Eleanor said, "what exactly were *you* doing in the King's bedchamber at that time of night, de Rathbone? It was *very* late."

"Why, my duty, of course," de Rathbone said smoothly. "I was merely checking on His Majesty's safety and security. Good job I did, too. Your husband was obviously planning to kill the King and take the crown!"

"Right, that's all I need to hear," said the King. "I hereby declare Bailey guilty as charged. Off with his head. In fact, off with all their heads, and be quick about it, will you? *I'll* die if I don't get something to eat soon. Um, quails' eggs and fried lampreys on toast, that's what I fancy..."

*Oh no*, thought Thomas, hardly able to believe what he had heard the King say, panic flooding through him. How could he save his family now?

Chapter Eight

# A Nickname Revealed

"*SEIZE THEM!*" roared de Rathbone, a look of total triumph on his face.

The crowd in the courtyard booed and surged forward and threw rotten vegetables. But the King's men held firm, and those guarding the Baileys grabbed them. Sir John protested, Lady Eleanor struggled, and Matilda knocked off a knight's helmet. Thomas suddenly found his voice.

"Your Majesty, please listen!" he yelled. "It wasn't Father planning to kill you, it was de

Rathbone. I heard him plotting in the Great Hall!"

The baron whirled round, eyes wide with shock and anger. Then he scowled. "The boy is lying!" he snarled. "Don't believe him, Sire!"

"Oh, do calm yourself, de Rathbone," said the King, airily waving his hand at him. "I don't believe a word of it. Carry on with the execution!"

The knights holding the Baileys pushed them onto their knees, and one of them produced a large axe. Thomas saw him checking the blade with his thumb, and wincing slightly when it drew blood.

Suddenly Thomas remembered something. He might be able to *prove* he had overheard the baron in the Great Hall...

He opened his mouth to speak, but Mother got there first. She glared at the knight holding the axe and he stepped back.

"Now just you wait a minute," said Lady Eleanor. "Nobody's being executed till I've had a word with my son." De Rathbone swore at her, but she ignored him. She turned to Thomas, raised a finely plucked eyebrow, and fixed him with a steely stare. "I'd like to know why you didn't tell us about this plot before dragging your father off to the King's chamber. Well? What have you got to say for yourself, young man? I'm waiting…"

"Sorry, Mother," said Thomas, thinking fast. He still didn't want to reveal the whole story. At least, not yet… "I was going to tell you, honest, but things have been, well, er…a bit complicated, and you were very busy, okay? Excuse me, but I really need to speak to His Majesty…"

"Complicated?" Mother said suspiciously. "What do you mean?"

"Yes, out with it, Thomas," Sir John said. "We won't be cross."

"Speak for yourself," said Lady Eleanor. "I probably will be."

"Uh-oh, little brother," said Matilda. "You're in trouble now."

"Oh, for heaven's sake, de Rathbone!" the King snapped at last. The courtyard had fallen silent, everyone listening fascinated to this exchange, even the baron and the rest of the King's bodyguards. "Can't you stop them talking?" said the King. "We'll be here all day at this rate!"

"Of course, My Lord!" growled de Rathbone, shaking his head and pulling himself together. He grabbed the axe and advanced on the Baileys with a deeply evil, murderous look on his face. "They'll soon stop their blather once I've sliced through their scrawny necks..." he muttered.

The crowd booed and surged forward again, led by Mouldy, and the King's men fell back.

Thomas gulped, and realized it was now or never.

"Er...excuse me, Your Majesty," he called out. "But is it true your parents didn't like you, and that your family nickname was...*Porky*?"

Now there was a great shout of laughter from the crowd, and even the King's bodyguards smirked. De Rathbone slowed down, his murderous expression changing into one of confusion. He stood still for a moment, frowning as he tried to take in what had just been said. Then his eyes grew *very* wide, and he raised his axe and made straight for Thomas.

"*NO!*" Mother and Matilda screamed, and Sir John yelled too and struggled against the knight holding him. But they needn't have worried.

"You can stop right there, de Rathbone," the King said coldly, and the baron froze in his tracks. "I have a question for the boy," added the King, turning to Thomas. "Now where did you hear that? It's not true, of course. Well, er...not exactly, anyway. And as for that stupid old nickname..."

"In the Great Hall, Your Majesty," Thomas replied. "As I said, I overheard de Rathbone plotting your murder. He said lots of awful things about you, and also that nobody else was supposed to know about you being called Porky. So if *I* know, then it must prove I'm telling the truth."

"The boy has a point, de Rathbone, doesn't he?" the King murmured, turning to stare balefully at the baron. "You're the only person to whom I've ever spoken about my childhood. So perhaps he's right, and you *are* plotting to kill me. What do you have to say for yourself?"

"Well done, Thomas," said Sir John. "You've really put him on the spot. Come on, de Rathbone! Let's hear your answer! We're all waiting!"

The crowd joined in, baying and hollering and calling out for the baron to reply, and the knights facing them suddenly looked uncertain. Thomas noticed De Rathbone's two henchmen quietly sidling over to join him.

"You want an answer?" de Rathbone said eventually, swinging the axe by his side and giving the King that cold, wintry smile again. "Here it is, then...*Porky*. Yes, I plotted to kill you and take the crown." There was a gasp of horror from the crowd, but de Rathbone ploughed on. "I've had enough of listening to you prattle on constantly about food, you stupid, ridiculous little man. I would make a *far* better King than you. And your reign would already be over if it hadn't been for that meddlesome brat and his fat fool of a father..."

"How dare you!" squeaked Lady Eleanor. "You're not fit to be my husband's footstool, you swine! And nobody calls my son a brat and gets away with it. You heard him Your Majesty... What are you going to do?"

"I'm going to have him arrested," said the King. "Seize him, men!"

Thomas smiled, sweet relief flooding through him. But de Rathbone wasn't defeated yet. Some

of the King's men moved towards the baron, ready
to do the King's bidding, although most stayed
right where they were, looking at each other and
the King and the baron in bewilderment.

"That's not going to happen," said de Rathbone
with a smug smile. "I think you'll find the men
know which side their bread is buttered on."

"Don't be ridiculous," said the King. "My men
will stay loyal to me!"

"Really?" said de Rathbone. "Well then, let's just see, shall we? *Ten gold pieces for every man who swears loyalty to...ME!*" he yelled.

A huge cheer went up from the bodyguards, and Thomas groaned.

Within seconds the King had been grabbed by de Rathbone's two henchmen and forced to kneel

beside the Baileys. The crowd seemed stunned, and
went quiet, the bodyguards easily pushing them
back now.

De Rathbone strolled up and down in front of the
Baileys and the King, smirking and idly swinging
the axe and enjoying his new-found power.

"Is there any chance that we could, er...talk about this, de Rathbone?" said Sir John. "I'm sure we could sort out our differences amicably."

"Oh, the time for talking is long gone," said de Rathbone, walking round to stand behind him. "And I'm not feeling very...*amicable* today."

He stopped beside Sir John and raised the axe, its wickedly sharp blade glinting in the sunlight. Lady Eleanor and Matilda screamed again, and Thomas quickly turned away. He simply couldn't bear to look.

But there were several more surprises in store for all of them...

# Chapter Nine

# Awesome Power

The first one came in the form of a large turnip

thrown by someone in the
crowd. It sailed through the
air and hit the knight
holding Matilda in the back
of the head with a...*CLANG!*
His helmet flew off, he went
totally cross-eyed, and he
slowly keeled over, much
to the crowd's delight.

Matilda immediately jumped up, ran over to de Rathbone, and kicked him as hard as she could in the knee, which came as rather a surprise to the baron. He squealed in pain and dropped the axe on his foot, hurting that, too. Soon he was

 hopping around, cursing and not knowing whether to hold his foot or his knee.

Seeing that there was a glimmer of hope, the crowd surged forward again, led as ever by Mouldy, and the knights retreated further this time. Mott was the next surprise. He bounded out of the crowd and made for the Baileys, barking wildly and snapping at the knights holding them. This distracted the knight behind Lady Eleanor, giving her the chance to thump him, while her husband tackled the knight in charge of Thomas.

"Run, Tom!" yelled Sir John, and Thomas did as

he was told, ducking past a couple of knights who
tried to grab him. The pushing and shoving
between the knights and the
crowd was turning into proper
fighting now, too. Swords
were brandished, helmets
were bashed, and the warm
air was filled with more
rotten vegetables than Cook
could have dreamed of.

Thomas ran out of the courtyard, and didn't
stop till he reached the northern wall. He stood by
the storehouse, panting and feeling desperate and

deeply guilty. His family
were in this mess because
of him, and even though
they were fighting back,
he didn't think they
stood a chance. Thomas
was sure de Rathbone
and the King's knights

would win in the end. After all, they were real soldiers, and no one could beat them...

Suddenly, Thomas realized that wasn't true. He had a secret weapon, a friend who could easily save his family. Sparky was bigger and stronger and scarier than de Rathbone or any number of knights. And what better way to show Mother how wonderful and loyal and sweet and incredibly *useful* a pet dragon could be? Thomas smiled. Things might work out well after all. But he'd better get a move on.

Thomas quickly pulled the storehouse doors open. Sparky's huge head appeared immediately,

 and he gave a loud moo-purr of pleasure. But he couldn't get his body through the doorway. So he retreated a little, then crashed forward, demolishing the

whole front wall of the storehouse, the rest of it soon collapsing behind him in a huge cloud of dust. Thomas's dragon rose to his full height, a creature of awesome power and beauty.

"Whoa!" said Thomas. His pet had doubled in size, at least. "Come on, Sparky," he said, remembering his mother's words on the day they had started preparing for the King's visit. "I've got a little job for you..."

Thomas ran off and Sparky followed, the ground shaking with every thundering step the great dragon took. When they entered the courtyard, the fighting stopped instantly and there was a sharp, collective intake of breath. Both sides looked up, their mouths wide open at this latest and greatest of all the surprises to happen in Creaky Castle that day.

"Right, Sparky, those three have been *really* horrible to

me!" Thomas said, pointing at de Rathbone and his two henchmen. "Go get 'em!"

Sparky stared at them for a moment, his head tipped over to one side, a slightly puzzled look on his face. Then he let out a hoarse chuckle...and fired off an enormous burst of flame. The baron and his men screamed and ran for their lives,

and almost everyone else in the courtyard did the same. Thomas, however, ran over to his family, and the four Baileys stood together, calmly talking while utter chaos whirled around them.

"I think you've got some explaining to do, Thomas," Mother said sternly, giving him her full-on, total-parental-disapproval frown. "I distinctly remember saying *no pet dragons.* So I'm assuming you secretly bought that appalling... *creature*, and have been keeping it hidden somewhere. I had a feeling you were up to something. Am I right?"

"Well...I suppose you are, technically speaking," said Thomas. "But I *was* going to tell you about Sparky as soon as I could, cross my heart..."

"*Sparky*?" snorted Matilda. "How did I know you'd come up with a totally lame name like that? Everybody calls their pet dragon *Sparky.*"

"I don't care what the animal is called," said Lady Eleanor, "you're not keeping it, okay?" Just then de Rathbone and his henchmen ran past the Baileys, still screaming, still pursued by the fire-breathing Sparky.

"But Mother, how can you possibly say that?" Thomas murmured. "I mean, without Sparky we'd be doomed. He's saving us from the baron!"

"I have to agree with Tom, dear," said Sir John.

"I don't really know how we would have coped without the dragon's, er...timely intervention. It certainly seems to have got old de Rathbone on the run, at any rate."

"Actually, I think it might be a bit bored with chasing the baron," said Matilda, who had been keeping a wary eye on what Sparky was up to. "And I hate to tell you, but I think it might be after somebody else..."

Thomas looked round, and groaned loudly. Sparky had given up on the baron and his henchmen and was happily chasing...the King. The dragon merrily ambled along behind him, letting the King stay a couple of steps ahead, even though it was obvious he could have caught him whenever he wanted. Occasionally Sparky fired off bursts of flame that scorched the King's

rear end. Each time the
King screamed in terror,
and tried to run faster.

Then Sparky caught
sight of the baron and
his henchmen and went
after them again, quickly
cutting off their escape route to the castle gates.

"Wonderful," moaned Mother. "The King really
is having the *perfect* stay with us. I only hope you
can get that beast under control, Thomas."

"Of course I can, Mother!" said Thomas,
although it turned out to be quite a bit harder
than he expected. Sparky was just *so* excited, like
a giant cat let loose among a flock of chicks or a
roomful of mice, and he seemed to want to chase
everybody, including the Creaky Castle servants.

But Thomas managed to calm him down
eventually, and together they concentrated on
penning the King's rebellious knights into a
corner of the courtyard, along with a terrified

de Rathbone and his two henchmen. Mouldy went over with the other Creaky Castle men-at-arms to help.

"Well done, Thomas!" said Sir John when the job was done at last.

"Yeah, pretty cool, little brother..." said Matilda. "I'm impressed."

"So, Mother," said Thomas, feeling confident. "What do you think of Sparky now? You have to admit he's been very...*helpful*, hasn't he?"

Mother opened her mouth to reply, but suddenly de Rathbone and his henchmen made a desperate break for freedom. Sparky growled, and chased them. They dodged one way, then another, and finally ran into the Keep, slamming the great doors shut behind them. Sparky paused...then he rammed the doors with his head, smashing them to splinters, and burst through. Thomas could hear him crashing around inside, destroying the furniture. Huge bursts of flame  came shooting out of the windows.

"*Helpful* isn't the word that springs to mind," groaned Mother. "And it was all so lovely after it was decorated..."

Thomas closed his eyes, certain he had just lost Sparky for ever.

Eventually, De Rathbone and his men ran out of the Keep, only to be recaptured by Mouldy and his lads. But even that couldn't make Thomas smile...

103

# Chapter Ten

# Something Original

Later that day, Thomas was sitting on the steps
up to the Keep, breathing in the smell of charred
wood and burned cloth wafting out through the
shattered doorway. Sparky lay beside him making
sad little mooing noises, gently nudging him from
time to time with his snout. But Thomas couldn't
be consoled. This was the gloomiest moment of
his entire life.

"I'm sorry, but that creature has got to go, and
the sooner the better," Lady Eleanor was saying

between sniffs, dabbing at her eyes with a hanky. "This is my *home*, and it's been ruined! I'll never get over it, *never!*"

She was standing with Sir John in the courtyard, supposedly supervising Creaky Castle's servants as they set about clearing up the awful mess that Sparky had made. There were scorch marks everywhere, and most of the buildings had been wrecked, including the stables and the barrack block. The interior of the Keep was, of course, *totally* devastated.

"I know how you feel, dear," said Sir John. "I'm upset too. But I sent Mouldy to the pet shop to ask if they'd take the dragon back, and they won't. And we can't just turn the poor thing out into the countryside, can we? I hardly think that would be very, er...responsible of us, would it?"

"I couldn't care less," said Lady Eleanor. "Either that creature goes – or *I* do!" She rounded on Thomas while Sir John spluttered. "And I don't know why *you're* sitting there doing nothing, young man..." she hissed.

"Because you told me to wait here while you tried to think of what else you could do to me, Mother," Thomas muttered. "Other than grounding me for life, that is, and making me get rid of the best pet I've ever had."

"It's the *only* pet you've ever had, isn't it?" said Matilda, coming out of the Keep with Mott. "Or will have now, probably. It's a shame you've got to lose him, though. I think it would be a lot of fun to have him around."

"There, you see, Mother!" said Thomas, surprised his sister was on his side. He felt a little surge of hope. "*Matilda* thinks we should keep him."

"Oh, *does* she?" said Lady Eleanor. "Well, *Matilda* isn't the one who gives the orders around here, is she? So she should just...keep...*quiet.*"

"Well, excuse me for daring to have an *opinion*," Matilda muttered.

"Listen, could we all stop arguing and try to calm down, please?" said Sir John. "I know, how about some lunch? I'm absolutely starving."

"We *can't* have lunch," said Lady Eleanor. "I fired Cook, remember? Although apparently he's still refusing to come out of the pantry."

"Ah, well, I er...wanted to talk to you about that, dear," Sir John said nervously. "Let's not be hasty. Cook has been with us a very long time..."

"Oh no, he *has* to go, just like the dragon," said Lady Eleanor. "He's a...a culinary catastrophe! The food here alone would have been enough to stop the King promoting you, even if none of the rest had happened."

"I have to say I think you're being rather unfair, dear," grumbled Sir John, frowning at his wife. "And where will poor Cook find another job?"

"That's not our problem, is it?" said Lady Eleanor. "What *we* need to worry about is coming up with the money to put things right here..."

Matilda joined in, agreeing with Father, and soon three of the Baileys were shouting at each other at the tops of their voices. Thomas sighed, and leaned against Sparky, his little surge of hope fading again. If only he could think of some way of persuading Mother to let him keep Sparky. But if it had been hard before, it seemed completely impossible now.

Suddenly Thomas heard the sound of hoofbeats, and the King came riding round the corner of the Keep, his bodyguard trotting along behind him. Baron de Rathbone and his two henchmen were on their horses, but their swords had been taken

away, and their hands were firmly tied to their
pommels. De Rathbone, however, looked
just as arrogant as ever.

The King reined in his horse
and halted his men. Sir John, Lady
Eleanor and Matilda stopped arguing, and
turned to face him, Mott sitting beside them.

Lady Eleanor blew her nose, patted her hair and smiled bravely. Thomas joined his family, and Sparky peered over their heads.

"Well, Bailey, I'm off, and not a moment too soon," the King muttered, shifting uneasily in his saddle, a spasm of pain passing across his face. His burned bottom must be quite sore, Thomas thought. "Staying here has been an absolute nightmare. You're lucky I don't have you hanged!"

"Er...I can't apologize enough, My Lord," Sir John said uncomfortably. "At least you can leave safe in the knowledge that you've put a stop to de Rathbone's plotting. I hope you'll devise a suitable punishment for him."

"I suppose you're right," said the King. "Although I'm not sure I can rely on my bodyguard to protect me from him. I had to promise them *twenty* gold pieces each for their loyalty, the greedy swines." Thomas glanced at the King's men, and noticed they had the grace to look a little sheepish. "As for punishing de Rathbone...I'd pay almost any price to the person who could suggest something original and *really* unpleasant."

"Hah! You don't frighten *me*," said de Rathbone, glowering at him.

Thomas scowled, and wished he could think of a punishment. Then several things came together in his mind all at once, and he felt as if a special ray of sunshine suddenly beamed down on him from above, and great choirs of angels appeared over his head and sang heavenly songs. It was the best idea anyone had ever had, the perfect solution to everything.

"Er...could I make a suggestion, Your Majesty?" he said, and all eyes turned to him. "I assume you'll be putting the baron in prison?" The King shrugged, and nodded. "Well, is there a cook for the royal dungeons? I only ask because *our* cook might be available, for the right fee, that is..."

"You mean...the man who made those *terrible* meals?" said the King, his eyes widening, a huge, joyful smile slowly creeping across his face.

"No, you can't!' moaned de Rathbone, *his* face a mask of horror and panic now. "It's...it's *inhuman*. I'm begging you, please, have mercy!"

"Silence, de Rathbone," said the King. "I think it's a *brilliant* idea. Well done, my boy. I'll have my treasurer sort something out with you, Bailey. Off we go, then. We can stop for lunch at an inn on the way. Cheerio!"

And so with a jaunty wave the King left Creaky

Castle, looking much happier than when he had arrived, Thomas thought. Now there was only one last loose end to be tied up. The most important one of all, though...

"With a bit of luck we should get enough to do all the decorating you want, Mother," said Thomas. "*And* have enough left over to keep a—"

"Um, it *would* be nice to tidy the place up again," said Mother. "I saw some *lovely* gold velvet hangings at The Drapes Superstore last week."

"I'd prefer it if you didn't use the word *hangings*, dear," said Sir John.

"*Gold velvet* hangings?" said Matilda. "I can't think of anything worse."

"HEY, WILL SOMEBODY LISTEN TO ME?" Thomas yelled at last. Lady Eleanor raised an eyebrow. "Er...sorry, Mother, I know I really shouldn't shout, but I need to know. *Can I keep Sparky or not?*"

Mother glanced at Father, who smiled and shrugged, and Matilda, who did the same. "Oh,

all right," Lady Eleanor said at last. "You deserve
it for making that nasty brute of a baron suffer.
But I'll be watching you *very* closely from now
on, young man, so you'd better behave yourself."

"Oh, don't worry," said Thomas, grinning at
Sparky. "I will."

But he had his fingers crossed behind his back
as he said it.

Everything you ever
wanted to know about
the author

Tony Bradman was a day-dreaming kind of
child – the sort of boy who always had his nose in
a book or pressed to the screen of his dirt-poor
family's ancient black and white TV. So it's no
surprise that he wanted to be a writer as soon as
he realized that such fabulous creatures existed.
Now, 200 books later, he dreams for a living, and
has found himself living the dream too – with an
85-bedroom mansion in the Beverly Hills of South
London, a garage full of gold-plated bikes,
publishers at his beck and call, and a job where he
only has to spend a couple of hours a day writing.
*(He can certainly dream, can't he? – Ed.)*

# Everything you ever wanted to know about the illustrator

Stephen Parkhouse wanted to draw ever since he was a toddler trying out new crayons on his bedroom wall. Mission accomplished, he now spends most of his life illustrating comic strips and graphic novels. He always liked the idea of becoming an author of children's books too, but having discovered how hugely difficult that is, he currently gets his writing fix by teaching Creative Writing at the Cumbrian Institute of the Arts.

Stephen lives in Carlisle, on the edge of Scotland and the Lake District, with assorted animals and family members.

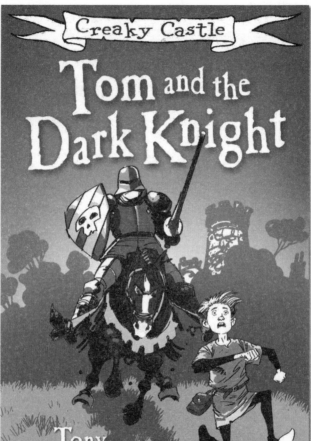

# Creaky Castle

# Tom and the Dark Knight

## Tony Bradman

Look out for more of mischief-maker
Tom Bailey's adventures!

# Tom and the Dark Knight

Tom has the biggest mouth in the kingdom and now he's put his foot right in it! Thanks to him, the terrifying Dark Knight thinks that Tom's father, the tubby, soft-hearted Sir John, is a champion fighter, and he's determined to smash him to pieces in Creaky Castle's Grand Jousting Tournament. How can Tom save his father without dropping himself into SERIOUS trouble?

Madcap schemes, thumping duels and fearsome foes...it's a medieval knightmare at Creaky Castle!

£4.99
ISBN 9780746072288
Coming soon...

For more action-packed tales of
mystery and mayhem
log on to
www.fiction.usborne.co.uk